W9-ABL-120

There's Nothing to Do!

by James Stevenson

Greenwillow Books, New York

Copyright © 1986
by James Stevenson
All rights reserved.
No part of this book
may be reproduced or
utilized in any form
or by any means,
electronic or mechanical,
including photocopying,
recording or by any
information storage and
retrieval system, without
permission in writing
from the Publisher,
Greenwillow Books,
a division of
William Morrow &
Company, Inc.,
105 Madison Avenue,
New York, N.Y. 10016.
Printed in Hong Kong by
South China Printing Co.
First Edition

10 9 8 7 6 5 4 3 2 1

Library of Congress
Cataloging in Publications Data

Stevenson, James, (date)
There's nothing to do!
Summary:
When Mary Ann and Louie
are bored, Grandpa tells
them what happened one day
when he and his brother
Wainey were bored.
1. Children's stories,
American.
[1. Boredom—Fiction.
2. Grandfathers—Fiction.
3. Humorous stories]
I. Title.
PZ7.S84748Tj   1986
[E]   85-8104
ISBN 0-688-04698-3
ISBN 0-688-04699-1 (lib. bdg.)

The illustrations are
full-color watercolors
combined with pen drawings.
The typeface is
ITC Clearface.

"It's never been *this* bad before," said Mary Ann.

"I can't stand another minute," said Louie.

"I think I'm going to scream," said Mary Ann.

"Me, too," said Louie.

"Scream?" said Grandpa. "What seems to be the trouble?"

"We're bored, Grandpa," said Louie.

"There's nothing to *do*," said Mary Ann.

"A bit quiet around here, eh?" said Grandpa.

"We *hate* being bored," said Louie.
"I know how it is," said Grandpa.
"I was once bored myself."
"You were?" said Mary Ann.
"When was that?" said Louie.
"I was about your age," said Grandpa.
"My little brother Wainwright and I
  were visiting our grandparents' farm.

Inside the house it was so still
you could hear the dust settle.

Outside, all day long,
the cows kept yawning.

The birds were so bored, they kept dozing off
and falling out of the trees.

One especially dull day, our grandparents went off to market.

Wainey started to cry.

Wainey was on top of the windmill.

Wainey landed in a wagon full of hay."

"The wagon started rolling downhill.
It went farther and farther.

I tried to catch up,
but I couldn't.

The wagon hit a fence."

"Wainey went flying into an enormous cornfield...

...and disappeared.

I went looking for him.

I searched for hours.

When I finally sat down to rest, I heard something coming.

It was Wainey riding a large pig.

Just then a bunch of bees arrived

...and stung the pig.

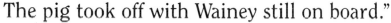
The pig took off with Wainey still on board."

"I followed the pig's trail through the barn. Then I heard a great splash!

The pig had landed in
the horse trough.

But where was Wainey?"

"Suddenly...

I was pulled backward farther and farther...

and lost my grip.

Wainey was gone.

A large mole had grabbed Wainey.

The mole went into a hole.

I could see the trail and hear Wainey's voice.

I dived in after Wainey and the mole

...and chased them."

"I saw Wainey and the mole running toward *me!*

They were being chased by a family of rabbits!

I followed them out of the tunnel."

"Not exactly. We went out on the porch to have our ice cream.
But just then the sky got dark and we heard a roaring sound.

We were lifted out of our chairs, and our ice cream blew away.

The twister carried us right through the house. It whirled us all around.

Suddenly the twister was gone.
Wainey and I fell down through the sky."

"Fortunately we landed in the
back seat of Grandpa's wagon.

WHAT'S NEW, WAINEY?
NOTHING MUCH! IN FACT, IT'S A LITTLE BORING OVER AT MY HOUSE!